THE IRON LAW

The Chronicle of the Fall

PRESTON GALT

(Translated from the Logbook of Marius, High Architect)

SIDERIS PRESS

The Chronicle of the Fall
(Translated from the Logbook of Marius, High Architect)
Preston Galt

Preston Galt
Published by Sideris Press

Printed Worldwide
First Printing 2026
First Edition 2026

10 9 8 7 6 5 4 3 2 1

ISBN: 979-8-218-92969-5

Library of Congress Control Number: 2026904997

A Note on the Text: This is a work of fiction. However, the laws of physics, economics, and thermodynamics described herein are non-negotiable. The failures of infrastructure, medicine, and logic depicted in Sideris are inspired by documented events. While the characters are products of the author's imagination, the collapse is real.

Cover Design: The Guild of Shadows

Editorial Review: The Office of Weights & Measures

Interior Book Design by Walt's Book Design

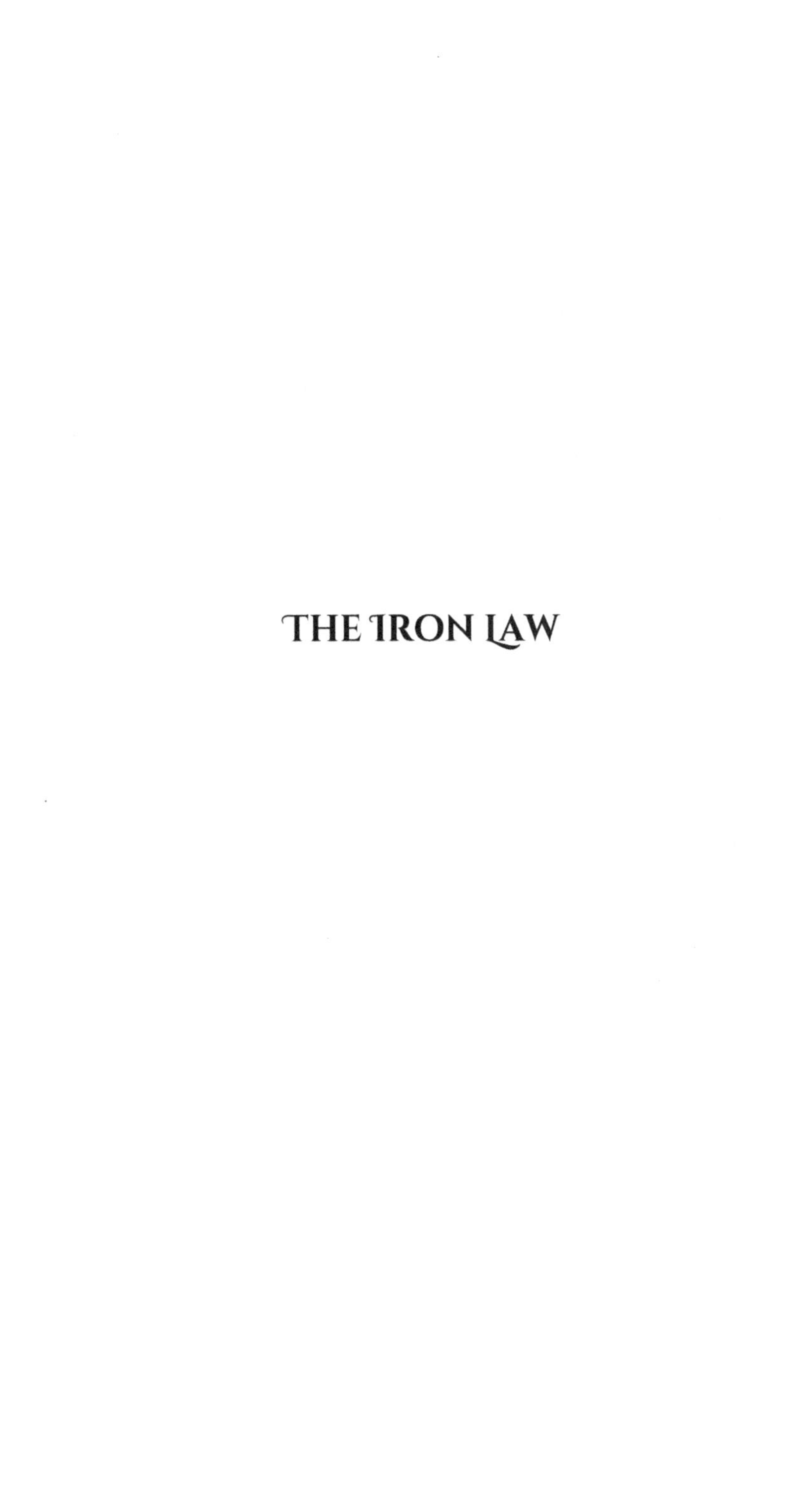

THE IRON LAW

DEDICATION

To the Mechanic who tightens the bolt when no one is watching. To the Surgeon who traded their youth for the skill to save yours. To the Lineman who climbs the tower in the storm. To the men and women who hold up the sky.

And to Morgan, Ari, and Michi. *May you never have to live in the dark.*

TABLE OF CONTENTS

INTRODUCTION

THE DEAD ZONE

I am writing this by the light of a fire made from currency. It burns green and purple, smelling of chemicals and broken promises. If you are holding this book, it means you still have electricity. It means the trucks are still running. It means you still have time.

I don't.

Three days ago, in the sub-basement of the ruined National Archives in what used to be Florida, I found a heavy iron box. Inside was the logbook of **Marius**, the High Architect of a city called **Sideris**. Historians will tell you Sideris is a myth. But as I translate Marius's words—struggling to read his terrified scrawl under the flickering light—I realize that Sideris is not a myth. It is a **mirror**.

Marius describes a civilization that didn't die from war or plague. It died because its leaders decided that **Competence was Cruel**. They decided that the laws of physics, biology, and economics were "exclusionary constructs" that could be repealed by a vote. They stopped testing their pilots. They stopped grading their doctors. They stopped arresting their thieves.

And then, one day, the physics filed a grievance. The gravity filed a lawsuit. And the lights went out.

I am publishing this translation not as a story, but as an **Autopsy**. Read it with your doors locked. And when you recognize the names, the laws, and the disasters in these pages... do not look away. Sideris is not a fantasy. Sideris is **Here**. And Marius is writing from the future you are currently building.

PART 1

THE DECAY OF THE BODY: PHYSICAL INFRA-STRUCTURE AND HEALTHCARE FAILURE

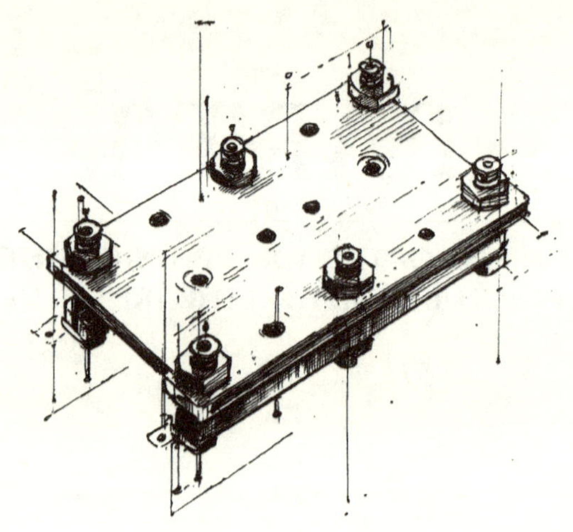

CHAPTER I

THE VIBRANCY AUDIT

48 HOURS TO ZERO.

The rot didn't start with a crash; it started with a "Day of Reflection."

I stood on the platform of the Iron Rail, watching the digital clock flicker and die. It was 08:00. The train was already twelve minutes late. In my pocket, my wrist-com buzzed with a Red Alert from the **Central Spire**: *Primary Cooling Intake at 88% capacity. Manual Override Required.*

I swiped the notification away, my jaw clenching. There was no way to initiate a manual override from a dead platform. I checked the time instead. 08:12. The schedule was slipping. It had been slipping for months, minute by minute, a slow-motion heart failure of the transit grid.

"Why aren't we moving, Marius?" **Jory** asked.

Jory was nineteen. He was a boy of the New City—soft hands, bright eyes, and a terrifying belief that the world was a vending machine that would dispense happiness if you pressed the right buttons. He wore his tunic loose, the collar unbuttoned, in the style of the poets. He looked like a victim waiting to happen.

"The train is late because the track is dirty," I said, pointing down into the dark trench of the rail bed.

In my youth, the Sanitation Guild swept the tracks before dawn. It was a ritual. A clean track meant a smooth contact for the induction wheels. It meant efficiency. It meant respect for the machine. But today, the rails were covered in a film of black grime, discarded wrappers, and the rotting husks of fruit. Rats moved in the shadows, their eyes reflecting the dim station lights. They were bold now. They sat on the third rail, grooming themselves, unafraid of a voltage that hadn't flowed properly in weeks.

"It's just trash," Jory shrugged, leaning back against a graffiti-covered pillar. "It doesn't weigh anything. The Crier said the Guild is having a 'Day of Reflection.' They're decolonizing the schedule. It's about time we stopped being slaves to the minute hand."

"Trash is friction," I snapped. I grabbed his shoulder—harder than I meant to. I felt the thinness of his bones under the fabric. If the grid failed, he wouldn't survive the winter. "Friction is heat, Jory. Heat destroys efficiency. If the wheel warps, the bearing seizes. If the bearing seizes, the train derails." I let go of his shoulder, turning back to the dark tunnel. "It's not just wrappers, Jory. It's a systemic failure of standards."

Jory pulled away, rubbing his shoulder, looking at me with a mix of annoyance and pity. "You always make it sound like a war, Marius. Maybe the sweepers just took a mental health morning. Rest is resistance."

"Resistance is maintenance," I muttered, letting him go. I rubbed my face, trying to hide my exhaustion. I was scaring him. But how could I not? I could hear the machinery of the city screaming, and he just heard the silence of a day off.

The train finally arrived, twenty minutes late. It didn't glide. It crawled into the station with a high-pitched, agonizing squeal—the sound of metal grinding on grit.

We took the rail to the Western District, to the great hangar of the Guild of Bo-Aeng. On the wall of the hangar, beneath a peeling motivational poster about "Inclusivity in Aerodynamics," someone had taped up an old schematic of a 737 Door Plug. It was yellowed with age. Over the diagram of the four critical retaining bolts, a red stamp had been pounded onto the paper: **REDUNDANT / REMOVED FOR WEIGHT EQUITY**.

I stared at the stamp. Ideally, those bolts held the pressure of the sky at bay. Now, they were considered dead weight.

We walked through the massive sliding doors, and the air hit me wrong. It didn't smell of hot metal, hydraulic fluid, and sweat. It smelled of lavender.

"They are masking the smell of the ozone," I whispered, the hair on my neck standing up. "Why are they perfuming a factory?"

The assembly floor was strangely quiet. There was no rat-a-tat-tat of rivet guns. Soft, ambient chimes played over the loudspeakers. The workers didn't march; they glided. They wore clean, white robes that looked more like vestments than coveralls.

I found **Harken**, the Master Wright. He was a giant of a man, carved from granite, sitting on a crate near the landing gear. He wasn't working. He was staring at his boots. His hands were shaking.

"Marius," Harken said. He didn't stand up. He looked smaller than I remembered. Defeated.

"I brought the boy," I said. "He needs to hear the rivet gun. He needs to learn the rhythm of the bond."

Harken laughed, a dry, bitter sound that rattled in his chest like loose gravel. "There are no guns, Marius. They took the compressors this morning."

"Took them?"

"The Council issued a directive," Harken said, reciting it from memory, his voice hollow. "'Percussive Assembly creates an Exclusionary Environment.' The noise was causing 'Auditory Trauma' to the administrative staff. It was aggressive. It made the writers feel unsafe. So, we switched."

"Switched to what?"

"**Chemical Bonding,**" Harken whispered, looking up with dead eyes. "Adhesive paste. It's silent. It's odorless. And it doesn't require a certification to apply. Anyone can do it. It's... inclusive."

I looked up at the wing. A young man in a purple sash was applying a white paste to a door plug. He wasn't measuring torque. He wasn't checking for gaps. He was smoothing the glue with a plastic spatula, like he was frosting a cake. He was humming, looking around to ensure he was being seen.

"The bolts were delayed," Harken said, his voice trembling. "But the launch window is absolute. If I stop the line, they audit my pension for 'Obstructionism'. I have a family, Marius. They threatened to rezone my housing."

We watched the launch from the observation deck. **Lysander**, the High Priest, gave a speech about "The Aerodynamics of Empathy." The ship rose on a pillar of blue fire.

For a moment, it was beautiful. It looked perfect.

And then, pop.

It wasn't a boom. It was the sound of a cork being pulled from a bottle.

At 16,000 feet, the pressure differential hit the door plug. The "inclusive" vanilla-scented glue failed. The door blew out. The Maximus didn't glide; it tumbled. It fell out of the sky like a stoned bird, spinning in a chaotic, terrifying dance toward the ground.

Jory gripped the railing, his knuckles white. "It... it fell. Why did it fall? They said it was built with love."

I watched the smoke rise from the distant crater. I didn't feel vindicated. I felt sick. I felt the cold realization that there was nowhere left to run.

"Physics doesn't care about love, Jory," I said, pulling him away from the railing before he could see the bodies. "It only cares about the bolts."

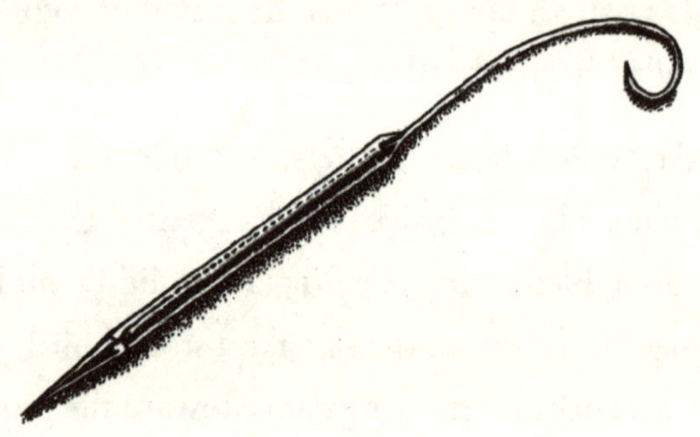

CHAPTER 2

THE HOUSE OF MEND

44 HOURS TO ZERO.

In the chaos of the stampede at the observation deck, **Jory** had fallen. He hadn't been pushed; he had simply tripped on a piece of rusted rebar jutting from the unmaintained concrete—a hazard that should have been cut and capped five years ago. It had sliced his forearm deep, flaying the skin back to the muscle in a jagged, ugly line. The blood was dark and venous, dripping steadily onto the floor of the train car as we fled, creating a sticky, rhythmic patter that seemed to count down the seconds of the city's life. *Drip. Drip.*

"We need a Healer," I said, my voice tight as I tied my own silk scarf around his arm. My fingers were slick with his blood, and for a moment, I fumbled the knot. I was the High Architect; I could calculate the load-bearing capacity of a suspension bridge in my head, but I couldn't tie a simple tourniquet without my hands shaking. "To the **House of Mend**."

The hospital was too warm. It didn't smell like the sharp, clean scent of antiseptic or the sterile bite of alcohol I remembered from my youth; it smelled of lilies and rot—the sickly-sweet smell of a funeral home disguised as a garden. The Triage Desk was manned by a **Wellness Guide** who was slowly sipping herbal tea and reading a pamphlet titled *The Vibrancy of the Spirit*. She didn't look up when we approached, even though Jory was pale and dripping blood onto her pristine, lavender-colored carpet.

"My apprentice is bleeding," I said, slamming my hand on the desk to shatter her trance. "He needs a Stitcher. Now."

"We do not call them Stitchers," she said, finally looking up with a soft, patronizing smile. Her eyes were glazed with a terrifying kind of calm. "They are **Tissue Aligners**. And you must wait. We prioritize based on Total Suffering." She pointed a manicured finger toward a healthy-looking man sitting in the corner, clutching a pillow. "This gentleman has a **Heavy Aura.** His spirit is bruised by the news of the crash. He requires immediate affirmation. Your boy merely has a physical laceration. Physical pain is transient. Spiritual pain is systemic. Please take a number."

I didn't take a number. I grabbed Jory by the collar of his tunic and kicked through the double doors leading to the surgical wing. We found **Valerius**, the last surgeon of the Old Guard, scrubbing his hands with a harsh, orange brush. His skin was raw and red from the friction, a stark contrast to the other "Aligners" in the hall who were simply putting latex gloves over unwashed hands.

"Ulnar side," Valerius grunted, casting a practiced eye at Jory's arm without stopping his scrub. "Missed the artery by a hair. Get him on the table and hold him down."

"Will you give me the numbing draught?" Jory asked, his voice shaking as he looked at the tray of steel instruments.

"**Lidocaine** was deemed 'Resource Intensive' by the Equity Board last quarter," Valerius said, drying his hands on a rough towel. "The entire stock was diverted to the Center for Comfort to treat generalized anxiety and 'Vague Unease.' We have none for trauma. Real pain gets nothing in Sideris." He handed Jory a thick leather strap, dark with the bite marks of a dozen men before him. "Bite on this, boy."

Valerius began to stitch the wound without anesthesia. The curved needle pierced the skin with a wet, popping sound, and Jory screamed—a raw, tearing sound that shattered the perfumed quiet of the hall. I felt his agony vibrate through my own shoulders as I pinned him to the table, my boots sliding in the blood on the floor.

Suddenly, the doors burst open. The **High Magistrate** was wheeled in on a gold-trimmed gurney, clutching his abdomen and howling in a way that had nothing to do with "Spirit Alignment."

"Appendix," Valerius said, his voice dropping an octave. "It's already leaking. Prep the theater! If we don't move now, he's a dead man."

"Stop!" A **Priest of Harmony** in a flowing purple robe blocked the path to the theater. "The Magistrate explicitly requested a Healer from the New Class in his directive. He requested the **Valedictorian**."

The Valedictorian was a boy barely older than Jory. He had never performed a live incision because the Academy had stopped the **cadaver labs** three years ago, claiming they were "undignified" to the deceased. He held the scalpel like a pen, his hand trembling as he looked at the Magistrate's belly. He hesitated, looking for a chart that wasn't there, and then he cut blindly. He went too deep. Blood sprayed the observation glass—bright, arterial red, a fountain of the Magistrate's life force hitting the floor.

Valerius didn't wait for permission. He shoved the boy aside so hard the Valedictorian hit the wall. Valerius plunged his bare, scrubbed hands into the open abdomen, finding the leaking artery by sheer, muscle-memory feel. He clamped it with his fingers, his face set in a grim mask of focus. He saved the man, but he did it with "aggression."

The next morning, before the Magistrate had even woken up, they fired Valerius.

"You created a **toxic environment**," the Inquisitor told him, standing in the middle of the bloodstained theater. "The patient's survival is not the only metric of a successful healing. You made the junior staff feel unsafe. You prioritized the result over the process."

As we left the House of Mend, Jory held his stitched arm close to his chest. The pain was etched into the lines of his young face, a shadow that hadn't been there yesterday.

"Marius," he asked quietly, his voice hollow. "If Valerius is gone... who stitches me next time?"

I looked back at the hospital, a cathedral of death masked by flowers and soft music. "No one, Jory," I said. "Next time, we just bleed."

CHAPTER 3

THE COIN OF FALSE PROMISES

The infection wasn't just in Jory's arm; it was in the very air of the city. As we walked toward the financial district, the wind carried the scent of Sideris's slow-motion rot—a cloying mix of expensive lavender perfume and the sour copper bite of stagnant gutter water. I looked at Jory, whose eyes were now rimmed with a sickly pink glaze of fever. For thirty years, I had taught my apprentices that the "Iron Law" was a shield, a way to keep the dark at bay through the cold, hard logic of the Riddle. Now, looking at the boy's trembling hands, I felt the crushing weight of a teacher's failure. I hadn't just failed to teach him how to build; I had failed to teach him how to survive a world that had traded its spine for "Community Joy."

We reached the **Vault of Silic**. Once, this lobby was a fortress of solvency, smelling of old leather and the sharp, ozone snap of high-end air filtration. Now, it smelled like a tomb. The air was thick and humid, trapped by a ventilation system that had likely been "de-prioritized" for a more equitable energy spend. Oily rainbows of chemical runoff shimmered in the puddles on the marble floor, reflecting the flickering holographic butterflies that danced above the High Aligner's desk like vultures over a corpse.

38 HOURS TO ZERO.

The fever was now undeniable. Jory's skin was hot to the touch, a dry, radiating heat that seemed to thrum against my palm when I checked his temperature. His breathing had become shallow and rhythmic, a soft whistle of air through teeth clamped tight against the pain of his arm.

"Antibiotics," I said, looking at the angry red streaks beginning to climb toward his elbow. "The House of Mend is a tomb. The pharmacy is empty. We need to buy from the black-market chemists in the Ash Waste, and they don't take promises. We need gold."

We went to the **Vault of Silic**, the financial heart of the city. A restless, shouting crowd was already pressing against the reinforced glass of the exterior doors, clutching their useless datapads. It was a massive, brutalist structure of granite and reinforced glass that used to represent the unshakeable stability of the Sideris economy. In my youth, entering this building felt like entering a temple; the air was cool, and the only sound was the hushed clicking of ledger keys and the heavy, reassuring thud of the vault doors.

I stopped at the water cooler in the lobby, my throat feeling as though it were lined with sandpaper. I was parched, and Jory needed fluids to fight the fever. I pressed the silver tab. The water didn't bubble with fresh air; it oozed. A thick, viscous stream of gray-green liquid trickled into the paper cup, smelling of stagnant ponds and old copper. The tank was scummy, coated in a layer of algae that looked like velvet.

"Don't drink it," I warned Jory, snatching the cup away. "They stopped changing the filters two years ago. The Water Council issued a decree that 'Pure Water' was a symbol of **Colonial Purity** that needed to be deconstructed for the sake of the environment. Now everyone drinks the sludge of the collective."

We ascended to the top floor, the elevator jerking and groaning on cables that hadn't been greased in a decade. We were there to see **Elara**, the High Aligner of Values. She didn't sit at a desk; she sat in a massive, purple beanbag chair in the center of an office filled with holographic butterflies. She was barefoot, swiping lazily through a datapad while sipping a neon-pink smoothie.

"I need my gold, Elara," I said, standing over her. I didn't care about the butterflies. "I have thirty years of credits stored in this Vault. My apprentice is sick, and I need the hard currency for the chemists."

"We don't do withdrawals of 'Hard Assets' anymore, Marius," Elara beamed, her eyes bright and unclouded by any understanding of the word *solvency*. "Physical asset extraction is a sunset model, Marius," Elara smiled, her tone perfectly even. "We transitioned the Vault's holdings into community-yield futures. The **Kite-Flyers**, for instance, offer a four-hundred percent return in localized wellness metrics. The ledger is perfectly balanced."

"Kite flyers?" I stared at her. "The Vault is supposed to hold the value of our labor. You traded the gold for... kites?"

"They aren't profitable in the traditional, 'oppressive' sense, obviously," she explained with a patronizing giggle. "But they generate massive amounts of **Community Joy**. We book that Joy as a liability offset on the ledger. It balances the books perfectly. By the math of the New City, we are the wealthiest generation in history."

"You can't buy antibiotics with a kite, Elara!" I roared. "What happens when the market turns? What happens when the people realize their savings are made of 'Community Joy'?"

"Joy is a stable currency," she said, her voice turning cold for the first time. "Our **ESG score** is a perfect 100. We have divested from everything heavy. Mining, steel, oil—it's all gone. We are a weightless bank for a weightless people."

Suddenly, a distant, muffled boom vibrated through the floorboards. Then came the sound of glass shattering downstairs—the visceral, unmistakable sound of a **margin call**. The mob had arrived. The rumor had finally reached the street: **The Vault is empty.**

We fled toward the back stairs as the alarm began to wail in a flat, unhurried tone. I looked back and saw men in expensive business suits fighting over the scummy water cooler, their faces twisted with a sudden, desperate thirst. Elara stood on the balcony, watching the riot below with genuine, heartbreaking confusion.

"Why are they angry?" she asked the empty room. "We were so nice to them! We gave them so much Joy!"

"The money is gone," Jory whispered as we ran down the concrete steps, his breath hitching in his chest. "The doctor is fired. The planes are falling. And the bank is full of paper."

"Yes," I said, shoving the exit door open into the chaos of the street. "No one is coming to save us, Jory. The cockpit is empty."

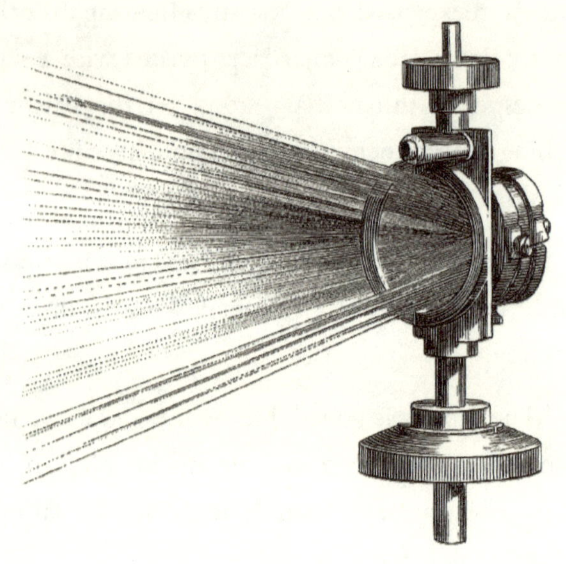

CHAPTER 4

THE WORKSHOP OF RATIOS

32 HOURS TO ZERO.

By the third morning, **Jory** could not make a fist. The swelling in his forearm had reached his elbow, the skin pulled tight and shiny like a piece of over-ripened fruit. He was burning with fever, his eyes glazed and unfocused, muttering about "perfect curves" and "iron bolts" that we would never find in this city of sand.

"We need a precision tool, Jory," I told him, forcing him to drink a few mouthfuls of the gray rainwater we had collected in a tarp overnight. "To escape the city and survive the **Ash Waste**, we have to have a high-precision surveyor's lens. Without it, we will die in the maze of the ruins before we ever see the horizon."

We walked to the **Artisan District**. In my youth, this sector was the beating heart of Sideris; it hummed with the constant whir of lathes, the high-pitched song of grinding wheels, and the sharp, clean smell of hot oil and shaved steel. But today, the street was silent. It felt like a graveyard where the monuments were rusted machines and the mourners were all in hiding.

We reached **Tobias's** Workshop, the premier glass-works in the district. The heavy oak door was blocked by two men in identical gray trench coats—**Inspectors from the Bureau of Ratios**. Inside, I could hear Tobias's voice, high and frantic, pleading with a third Inspector who stood calmly with a clipboard.

"I hired the boy because he can feel a micron variance with his eyes closed!" Tobias shouted, his voice cracking with desperation. "He is the only one who can grind a lens for a deep-space sextant!"

"It does not matter," the Inspector said, his voice as flat and unyielding as a stone. "By hiring the 15th man, you have crossed the **Threshold of Compliance**.

You are no longer a small artisan shop; you are a Tier 1 Enterprise. Fourteen of your men are from the **Stone Clan**. That is **Legacy Bias**. To be compliant, you must immediately hire from the **River Clan** until you reach the Ratio. Until then, your workshop is under a Work-Stop Order."

Tobias went pale. He looked at his machines, then at his men. To save the shop, he had to fire his best. He turned to his lead grinder, **Karn**, a man who had spent twenty years perfecting the art of the curve.

"Karn," Tobias choked out, unable to meet the man's eyes. "I'm sorry. The Bureau says I have no choice."

Karn didn't argue. He didn't shout. He simply took off his heavy leather apron, folded it neatly on his workbench, and walked out into the gray street—a master of his craft made obsolete by a demographic spreadsheet.

The Inspector gave a sharp whistle, and five drifters who had been leaning against a nearby wall stepped into the shop. They were young, their tunics clean and unsoiled by the dust of the wheel.

"These are your new **Senior Grinders**," the Inspector announced.

One of the new men sat at Karn's station. He didn't inspect the grain of the glass; he didn't even check the speed of the wheel. He jammed a raw slab of optical glass against the diamond tip without cooling fluid. The friction heat cracked the glass instantly, sending a spray of shards flying across the room like shrapnel.

"Oops," the man said, shrugging his shoulders as he wiped a speck of dust from his tunic. "This machine is stupid. It's not intuitive at all."

Tobias fell to his knees, picking up the jagged pieces of the lens that was supposed to guide a ship through the stars. "It is over," he whispered. "The lenses will be blurry. The ships will hit the rocks. The light is being bent by fools."

I reached onto the shelf and grabbed the last surveyor's transit Karn had finished before the inspectors arrived. I pressed a handful of credits into Tobias's shaking hand.

"Come, Jory," I said, leading the boy back out into the silence of the district.

"Don't ever buy a pair of glasses from this city again. They can no longer see the truth, let alone grind it into glass."

PART II

THE DECAY OF THE MIND: EDUCATION, TRUTH, AND LOGIC

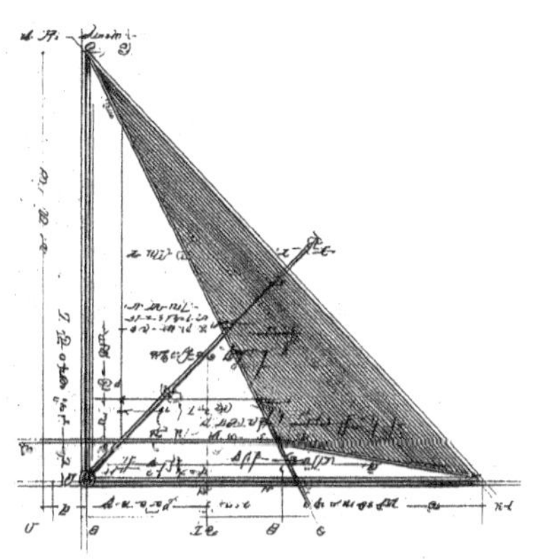

CHAPTER 5

THE BANISHING OF THE RIDDLE

26 HOURS TO ZERO.

The air was getting colder as the sun dipped behind the jagged silhouette of the Central Spire. We climbed the Thousand Steps to the **Academy of Vectors**, the ivory towers that had once been the repository of all human logic. Jory was leaning heavily on my shoulder now, his breath hitching with every upward step.

The Great Library, once a sanctuary of vellum and ink, felt hollow. Its shelves were largely bare, stripped of the heavy volumes on calculus and structural load-bearing that had defined my own education. The remaining scrolls were thin, decorative things with titles like *The Geometry of Kindness* and *Vectoring Inclusivity.*

Thaddeus, the High Mathematician, emerged from the shadows of a vacant alcove. He looked like a man made of glass—fragile, translucent, and ready to shatter.

"They've taken the primers, Marius," he hissed, his eyes darting toward the hallway where the sound of rhythmic chanting drifted from a classroom. "The Council decided that the concept of a 'Right Answer' is a form of intellectual oppression that discourages the vibrance of the marginalized. They call it **De-tracking.** We are no longer allowed to teach the Riddle."

I looked into the nearest lecture hall. Students were sitting in a circle on plush beanbags, eyes closed, discussing their "emotional journey" with triangles rather than solving for the hypotenuse.

"If they don't know the hypotenuse, the roof collapses," I whispered.

"The roof is a 'Legacy Concern,'" Thaddeus replied with a bitter smile.

We moved toward the **Scale of Entry**, the gate where the next generation of builders was being selected. A boy from the Stone Clan—a boy with calloused hands and a mind like a razor—placed his **Knowledge Stone** on the scale. It was a perfect test score, the weight of his merit clear for all to see.

But the Proctor, a woman in a flowing silk robe, didn't look at the score. She reached into a velvet bag and placed a lead weight on the opposing side of the scale labeled **Personality Adjustment**.

"The Stone Clan lacks **Vibrancy**," the Proctor announced to the room. "He is too rigid in his thinking. He prioritizes the result over the 'Social Harmony' of the workspace. We must consider the 'Whole Student' to ensure a balanced future."

The boy's side of the scale rose, effectively rejecting him. In his place, a boy from the River Clan with a failing score was admitted. The Proctor added a massive weight labeled **Heritage Bonus** to his side, forcing the scale down until it hit the table with a dull thud.

Suddenly, the great bronze bell of the Academy rang—the **Purge**. The faculty was lined up in the courtyard, their shadows long and thin against the white stone. On one side were the **Grey-Beards**, the men and women who held the blueprints of the city's heart. On the other was the **New Class**, hired for their "Alignment" with the Council's vision.

"Logic dictates you fire the newest!" I shouted from the stairs, my voice echoing through the silent courtyard. "They have no experience!"

The High Priest of the Academy stepped forward. "In Sideris, **Equity supersedes Seniority**," he said. "The seniors represent a 'Legacy of Exclusion.' Their very knowledge is a barrier to the new vibrance we are cultivating. We are pruning the old to let the new light in."

I watched in silence as guards stripped the academic robes from the old men, including Thaddeus. He didn't fight them. He simply reached into his tunic and shoved a small, leather-bound geometry book into my hands.

"Hide it, Marius," he whispered, his voice cracking. "The light of the Riddle is going out. Soon, no one will know how to measure the dark, and they will call the darkness progress."

CHAPTER 6

THE GUILD OF SHADOWS

20 HOURS TO ZERO.

The public cisterns were dry, their stone basins cracked and dusty under the fading light. "The Council froze the deployment of the repair crews until the 'Humanity Ratio' was met," I told Jory as we passed a line of people waiting with empty buckets. "They would rather the city thirst than be served by a crew that doesn't reflect the 'Vibrancy' of the district."

We reached the job site of the **Great Span**, the bridge that was supposed to connect the industrial heart to the shipping ports. In my youth, a project of this scale would have been an engine of industry—a forest of iron scaffolding and the constant, rhythmic heartbeat of steam-hammers. Instead, the site was eerie and quiet. In the center of the construction zone, where the primary load-bearing pylon should have been rising, stood a single, luxurious tent made of royal purple silk.

Inside the tent, the air was thick with the scent of jasmine and expensive tobacco. **Varon**, the High Contractor, was reclined on a mountain of velvet pillows, a crystal flute of pale wine in his hand. He didn't look like a builder; he looked like a poet who had never felt the weight of a wrench.

"The bridge is in the **Community Listening Phase**," Varon said, his voice smooth and untroubled by the deadline. "We are 'decolonizing' the architecture. The original plans were too 'assertive.' Those straight lines and sharp angles lacked fluidity and made the River Clan feel excluded. We are redesigning the Span to be more... conversational."

"You spent the concrete budget on a tent and a 'listening phase'?" I roared, my voice echoing off the silent machinery. "The city needs transport, Varon! Not a redesign of the hypotenuse!"

"Innovation requires overhead, Marius," he sighed, waving a hand dismissively. "We are cultivating a space of equitable transit, Marius. The concrete is secondary to the social impact."

I left the tent and walked down into the mud of the foundation pit, where the real work was hidden from the street. There, in the shadows, I found **Kael** and a dozen men from the Stone Clan. They were mixing concrete by hand in rusted buckets, their backs bowed under the weight.

"We are forbidden from the official contract," Kael spat, wiping grit from his eyes. "The Council says we lack the 'Relational Intelligence' to work in the sun. So Varon pays us scraps to do the work in the dark. We are his **Ghosts**. He takes the credit for the 'Conversational Span,' and we do the math he can't understand."

I knelt and touched the pylon they were pouring. I didn't need a lab to know what I was feeling. The mixture was thin, watery, and gritty with unwashed river sand.

"It won't hold, Kael," I said, my heart sinking. "The cement-to-aggregate ratio is a joke. It'll crumble under its own weight before the first wagon crosses."

"I know," Kael whispered, his voice cracking with a mix of shame and exhaustion. "But we need the credits to eat. The bridge is a lie, Marius. It's a political monument made of dust. It will fall the moment the first heavy load hits the center, and Varon will blame the 'Assertive' physics of the past."

I stood up and looked at Jory, who was leaning against a rusted crane, his face pale in the twilight.

"We have to find another way out," I told him, gripping his shoulder. "The ground is literally giving way beneath us, and the men at the top are still debating the 'vibe' of the collapse."

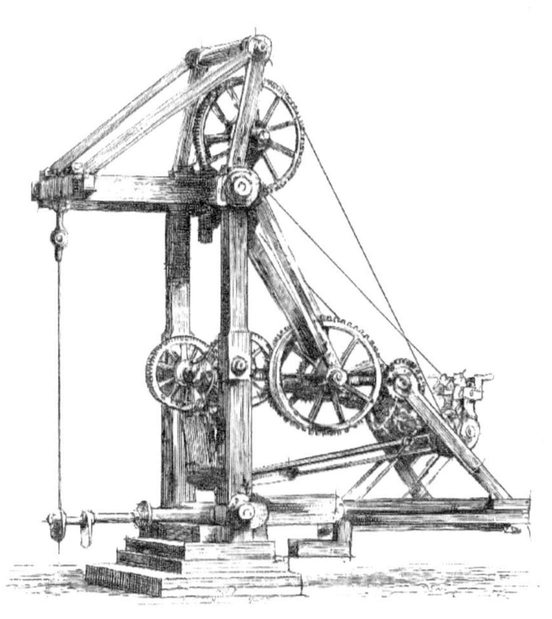

CHAPTER 7

THE HEAVY LADDER

14 HOURS TO ZERO.

The **Library of Records** was burning. It was a slow, heavy fire that tasted of ancient parchment and ozone. Smoke rose in a black, oily pillar that seemed to prop up the gray sky of Sideris. This wasn't just a building; it was the city's memory—blueprints of the Great Dam, the treaties of the Founders, the original cooling schematics for the Spire—all turning to white ash that drifted over the cobblestones like snow.

A crowd had gathered at the perimeter, but they weren't helping. They stood like ghosts, their faces lit with a ghoulish orange glow, holding up their digital slates to record the destruction. No one reached for a bucket. No one shouted for the watch.

The fire wagon finally arrived, its brass bells clanging with a hollow, frantic sound. But the recruits moved with a terrifying hesitation. **Ash**, the Fire Chief—a man whose face was a map of burn scars and thirty years of service—roared for the primary hose to be deployed.

Two recruits grabbed the brass nozzle. It was a heavy, industrial-grade piece of equipment designed to withstand the pressure of a city main. As they pulled it toward the blaze, they stumbled. The hose coiled in the mud, lifeless.

"It's too heavy!" a recruit shouted, his voice cracking with panic as he dropped the nozzle.

"Pick it up!" Ash screamed over the roar of the flames. "The pressure is coming! If you don't hold it, it'll whip and kill us all!"

"We have **vertical exertion waivers**!" the recruit yelled back, pointing frantically to a badge pinned to his yellow tunic. "The new standards say we don't have to lift more than fifty pounds. This hose is 'exclusionary'! It wasn't designed for our demographic comfort!"

A woman appeared at a third-story window, her silhouette framed by a halo of fire. She was screaming, her hands clawing at the glass. Ash ordered the iron ladder to be deployed. It was a massive, hand-cranked relic of the Old World. The recruits lifted it barely three feet before their knees buckled.

"I can't!" one wailed, letting the iron rail slip. "My alignment is off! This task is a grievance against my well-being!"

They dropped the ladder with a sickening, metallic thud that echoed off the burning walls.

Ash and I—two old men who still remembered the weight of iron—grabbed the rails ourselves. My joints popped, and the heat from the building felt like it was peeling the skin from my forehead. We heaved it into the air, the cold metal biting into our shoulders. We slammed it against the sill just as the window melted into a stream of liquid glass.

But it was too late. The woman vanished into a localized sun of orange and white. The floor had given way.

"The fire audits everyone, Marius," Ash said, wiping soot from his brow as we watched the roof collapse. "It doesn't care if you passed the new test or if they just gave you the badge to fill a quota. If you can't lift the ladder, the building burns. The physics doesn't recognize a waiver."

CHAPTER 8

THE EQUITY ALGORITHM

8 HOURS TO ZERO.

The auto-tram didn't glide; it suffered. As the glass capsule lurched forward, the magnetic rails emitted a sickly, high-pitched whine—a mechanical groan that sounded like a living thing being slowly crushed. The air inside was stale, smelling of ozone, burnt copper, and the unwashed desperation of the few passengers left. I watched the city blur past the scratched windows, a landscape of grey concrete and neon slogans that had lost their glow. I found myself thinking back to the Academy, to the way the "Riddle" used to be taught as a foundational truth rather than a legacy to be deconstructed. I looked at Jory's pale face and wondered if the city had forgotten how to fix the magnets for the same reason it had forgotten how to value a human life: because both required a precision that the new world found offensive.

Jory was fading. His breathing was shallow, a wet, rattling sound that made my chest tighten with every step. We boarded an **auto-tram**, a glass capsule moving on magnetic rails that should have whisked us to the black-market chemists in minutes.

The tram lurched, accelerated for three blocks, and then stopped dead at an empty intersection.

"Why are we stopping?" Jory asked, his voice barely a whisper.

A **Coder** in a purple tunic sat at the control terminal in the front of the car, watching bar graphs scroll across a blue screen. "We are in a **Latency Injection** cycle," he said without looking up. "The algorithm detected we were moving 40% faster than the average pedestrian traffic on the lower levels. That creates a 'Velocity Gap.' It's inequitable for some to arrive at their destination while others are still walking in the rain."

"But there are no pedestrians!" I shouted, slamming my fist against the glass. "Look at the street! It's empty! And I have a dying boy here!"

"Physical presence is irrelevant to the systemic math," the Coder replied, his voice flat and perfectly reasonable. "By pausing the tram, we ensure the 'Speed-Privileged' do not reach their goals at the expense of the 'Stationary Class'. It's called **Democratizing the Destination**. We are evening the field."

A block away, a medical ambulance was trapped behind a stationary freight hauler. Its lights flashed—a frantic, rhythmic red—but its siren was silent.

"The Council removed the sirens last month," the Coder said, almost to himself. "High-decibel alerts suggested that one person's emergency was more significant than the collective's peace of mind. It gave the patient a 'Main Character Syndrome' that was deemed socially disruptive. Now, everyone waits their turn in silence."

The ambulance lights flickered and then went dark.

I watched the paramedics step out, shoulders slumped, as they began to fill out paperwork on their slates. The patient had died in the quiet of the afternoon while the Coder balanced his graphs.

PART III

THE DECAY OF THE SOUL: FAMILY, JUSTICE, AND THE FINAL MECHANICAL COLLAPSE

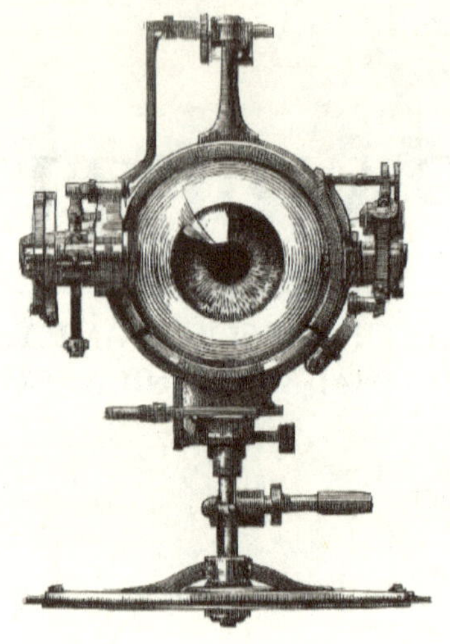

CHAPTER 9

THE NURSERY OF SPIES

4 HOURS TO ZERO.

The rain was turning to sleet, a freezing drizzle that turned the cobblestones into a mirror of the city's gray soul. We reached the house of **Tomas and Elena**—old friends who still remembered how to read a blueprint. They taught their seven-year-old daughter, **Sia**, the truth in the basement by candlelight.

But as we entered, Sia wasn't looking at her father. She was staring at her state-issued datapad. A cartoon owl blinked on the screen, its eyes wide and friendly. *Did your parents make you feel unsafe today?* the owl asked in a high, chirping voice. *Did they use words that weren't in the Daily Lexicon?*

"The Crier said there is no fire at the Library," Sia recited, her voice a flat monotone. "He said it was a 'thermal celebration of transitional history.'"

"Use your eyes, Sia," Tomas said, his voice trembling. "You can see the smoke from the window."

Sia looked at her father with a terrifying, clinical pity. "The Teacher said parents suffer from 'Reality Distortion' due to their Legacy Bias," she said softly. She tapped her screen three times. *Ding-Ding-Done.*

"What did you do, Sia?" Elena whispered, her face going white.

"I helped Papa get better," Sia said. "I submitted a **Concern Report**."

Ten minutes later, the front door was kicked open. Agents from the **Sept of Care** arrived. They didn't carry weapons; they carried "Stabilization Nets."

"We received a report of Intellectual Danger," the lead agent said, checking a slate. "A failure to affirm the collective narrative. Tomas, you are required for 'Perception Realignment.'"

Sia stood up and walked to the agent, taking his hand. "He burned a book in the fireplace," she told him. "A book with numbers in it."

"She belongs to the Future now," the agent said, leading the child away. Tomas and Elena were forced into a separate van.

"They turned her into a camera," Elena wailed as the door slammed shut.

I dragged Jory back into the freezing rain, ducking into an alley as the sirens—the few that remained for the State—began to wail. The walls had ears, the children had datapads, and the truth was now a crime against the "Safety" of the lie.

CHAPTER 10

THE BLIND SCALE

2 HOURS TO ZERO.

We were fugitives now, moving through the narrow veins of the city where the stagnant water reflected the flickering, dying streetlights in oily rainbows. Jory was deteriorating rapidly; the infection had crossed the threshold into his blood, and he moved with the heavy, jerky gait of a man walking through deep mud. He stumbled, his fingers white-knuckled as he clutched a heavy iron fire-poker we had scavenged from a ransacked hearth—our only weapon against the scavengers and the wolves.

The **Bridge of Judges** loomed ahead, a massive stone span that served as the final checkpoint before the industrial gates. It was manned by **Peace Guides** in pastel blue vests, their faces hidden behind polished glass visors. They didn't carry swords; they carried catch-poles and weighted nets.

"Drop the implement," a Guide said, his voice amplified by a throat-mic until it vibrated in my teeth. The iron poker clattered onto the cobblestones with a cold, lonely sound.

The **Magistrate** sat at a folding table in the center of the bridge, his face lit by the blue glow of a terminal. "Marius the Architect," he murmured, his eyes scanning my file. "Charged with 'Aggressive Loitering' and 'Possession of a Kinetic Multiplier'."

A figure stepped from the shadows behind the table—**Kaelo**, a known member of the street gang that had sacked the Watch Station three nights prior. He was wearing a stolen officer's sash, but the Magistrate treated him like a dignitary.

"This is Kaelo," the Magistrate said, gesturing to the thief. "He claims your associate—this boy—caused him 'Spiritual Distress' during a resource acquisition."

"He burned the bakery!" Jory rasped, his voice cracking. "He took the bread from the mouths of the hungry!"

"He was engaging in **unsanctioned resource redistribution due to historical scarcity**," the Magistrate corrected, not looking up from his screen. "You, Marius, have had the privilege of the Spire. The scales must tip to achieve Harmony. The judgment is **Restorative Transfer**."

The Guides didn't strike me; they simply stepped forward and ripped the heavy wool coat from my back. One of the Guides tossed it to Kaelo, who buttoned it slowly, his eyes locked on mine with a smirk. Then, another Guide reached into Jory's pocket and pulled out the last tin of antibiotic ointment we had bartered for with our final credits.

"Unauthorized possession of high-value chemistry is theft from the collective," the Guide recited. He handed the tin to Kaelo, who didn't even open it. He simply flicked it over the railing and into the black, rushing river below.

"Case resolved," the Magistrate said, tapping a key. "Go with grace. And remember: individual survival is a grievance against the whole."

CHAPTER II

THE COLD FURNACE

0 HOURS.

The **Turbine Hall** loomed before us like the hollowed-out ribcage of a fallen god. It was the absolute heart of Sideris, the place where the laws of thermodynamics were supposed to be the only authority. Inside, the **Great Wheel** was grinding—a sick, rhythmic *Ka-thunk* that shook the very bedrock of the city.

Proctor Elian scrambled down the metal stairs, his white robes stained with oil and his eyes wide with a frantic, narcissistic terror.

"Marius! The vibration is shaking the foundation!" Elian begged, clutching at my sleeve with trembling hands. "The Council says the noise is an 'Aggressive Sonic Environment,' but the machines won't listen! If the Wheel stops, the heating grid fails. The poets in the Upper Spire will freeze in their sleep!"

"The governor valve is stuck open," I shouted over the roar of the dying turbine, my voice raw. "The steam pressure is red-lining. I need a mechanic on the high catwalk to pull the manual release lever!"

"The catwalk is 'Safety Restricted'!" Elian shrieked back. "My men have sensory issues with the height, and the railing hasn't been certified for 'Inclusive Access'! No one will go up there!"

"I'll go," Jory said, his voice dropping the slur. He pushed himself off the wall, his eyes bright with a terrifying, terminal clarity. His face was the color of wet ash, and his body was shaking with a fever that was burning through the last of his reserves. He looked at the ladder, then at me. It wasn't strength moving him now; it was the final, desperate adrenaline of a dying man who knows he has exactly one task left to complete. There was a spark in his eyes I hadn't seen since the crash—the spark of a builder who finally understood that the machine didn't care about his feelings.

"Stop!" Elian shouted as Jory reached for the first rung. "He cannot ascend without the **Vestment of the Gear**!"

Elian pulled a heavy purple velvet robe from a glass case, draped with a long, shimmering gold sash that trailed three feet on the floor. "The Council decreed that all manual labor must be performed with **'Visual Dignity.'** This garment represents the honor of the collective."

"That sash is a death sentence!" I yelled, trying to rip the fabric away. "Loose clothing near a high-speed flywheel violates the **First Law of Safety**! It'll snag the axle!"

"Standards are a legacy of the unfeeling past!" Elian countered, wrapping the robe around Jory's shivering frame. "He must be draped in dignity!"

Jory was blue with the creeping cold of the hall, and the robe looked warm. In that moment, exhausted and desperate to save the boy from the chill, I hesitated. I allowed the immediate need for comfort to override the hard physics I had taught for thirty years. **I broke my own law.**

"Put it on, Jory," I whispered. "Just be careful."

Jory climbed. He hauled himself up one rung at a time, his breath rattling in his chest like loose gears. When he finally reached the high catwalk, he didn't pause. He grabbed the manual release lever and pulled it with a scream of effort that sounded like metal shearing. The valve hissed; the steam vented into the night sky, and the engine hum began to smooth into a steady, safe purr. He turned to smile at me from the height, the gold sash catching the artificial light.

Then, the wind from the spinning flywheel shifted.

The long, golden sash fluttered for a fraction of a second before it was sucked into the rotating housing of the primary axle.

CRUNCH.

Jory didn't even have time to scream. The velvet robe acted as a net, dragging his slight frame into the gears with the speed of a falling hammer.

Blood erupted from the casing in a hot, dark mist, drenching Elian's white robes and the brass controls of the dead city. But the **Great Wheel** did not stop immediately. A machine of that scale possesses a terrifying, unyielding momentum. It ground forward, the heavy iron teeth of the primary axle violently stripping themselves as they choked on the sudden, foreign mass of fractured bone and shredded fabric.

For ten agonizing seconds, the **Turbine Hall** filled with the deafening shriek of shearing metal—a sound like the hull of a deep-sea vessel buckling under the crushing weight of the ocean. The governor valve blew entirely, venting a massive, blinding cloud of high-pressure steam into the rafters. The smell of burning oil and copper flooded the cold air.

Then, finally, the torque failed.

The **Great Wheel** groaned, shuddered, and died. The immense silence that followed was heavier than the noise had ever been. The lights in the hall flickered once, twice, and then went completely black.

The Future was dead, suffocated by its own mandated vestments, leaving us in the absolute dark.

CHAPTER 12

THE EXODUS

I sat in the absolute silence of the Turbine Hall. **The absence of the hum was heavier than the noise had ever been. It pressed against my eardrums—the sound of a heart that had stopped beating.** The only sound was the rhythmic drip of cooling oil onto the stone floor and the distant, fading echo of Elian's footsteps as he fled toward the upper levels to find a mirror. I didn't look at the gears. I didn't look at what remained of the boy who had believed in a world built with love.

I stood up, my knees popping with the sound of dry twigs. I walked toward the exit, carrying nothing but the small, leather-bound volume of geometry Thaddeus had pressed into my hands. My coat was gone, my apprentice was dead, and my city was a cold tomb of purple velvet and "Community Joy."

I walked through the streets of Sideris one last time. The darkness was total. Without the induction rails, the commuters were huddling in the stations, their digital slates glowing like dim, blue ghosts as they waited for a "Latency Injection" that would never end.

I reached the **Old Foundry** at the edge of the city. There, by the dormant furnaces that had once forged the spine of the world, I found the others. They were waiting in the shadows: **Valerius**, his hands still stained with the Magistrate's life; **Tobias**, clutching a single, cracked lens; **Ash**, the Fire Chief, and the **Ghosts** of the Stone Clan.

We didn't speak. There were no more words in the Daily Lexicon for what we had to do. We simply turned our backs on the Spire and began to walk.

We walked until the air grew sharp and the smell of lavender was replaced by the honest, biting scent of pine and wet earth. We walked until we reached a clearing at the edge of the tree line, miles from the corpse of the city.

Valerius struck a flint. He didn't ask for a waiver or a "Day of Reflection." He simply struck the steel against the stone until a small, orange flame sparked to life in a nest of dry needles. It wasn't a "thermal celebration." It was a fire. It was hot. It was real. And it followed the laws of the universe.

"Where do we go, Marius?" Thaddeus asked, looking at the geometry book in my hand.

I looked at the fire, and then I looked up at the stars—the same stars the Academy had stopped counting because their distance was deemed "exclusionary."

"We go to a place where the bolt breaks if it is loose," I said, my voice steady for the first time in years. "We go to a place where the sash is forbidden and the truth is the only currency."

"We start again."

EPILOGUE

THE AUTOPSY OF THE FUTURE

The logbook of Marius ends there.

I found it in the iron box, protected from the rot that claimed everything else in that dead zone. As I close the cover, I can hear the hum of my own city outside my window. I can hear the news reports of "Velocity Gaps" and "Resource Redistribution." I can see the "Wellness Guides" replacing the doctors and the "Coders" replacing the engineers.

Sideris did not fall in a day. It fell one waived standard at a time. I see the blueprints of this doomed city every time a commercial airliner loses a door plug at 16,000 feet because quality control was marginalized. I see it when a state's power grid freezes solid because winterization was deemed a legacy expense.

Sideris isn't a myth; it's a mirror. It fell because the people who knew how to hold up the sky were silenced by the people who wanted to redesign the clouds.

The fire I am writing by is low. The green and purple flames of the old currency are almost out. But I have the book. I have the math. And I have the warning.

The Iron Law is coming for us all. And when it arrives, it won't care about your "Vibrancy." It will only care if the bolt holds.

Build accordingly.

— Preston Galt

APPENDIX

THE AUTOPSY REPORT

The following records serve as the historical precursors to the collapse of Sideris. These are not fables; they are the documented instances where the laws of physics, economics, and biology were ignored in favor of the Narrative.

I. The Engineering Failure: Structural Decay

- **The 737 MAX 9 Mid-Air Blowout (2024):** A door plug was ejected during flight because four critical retaining bolts were missing after a "quality intervention." This mirrors the "**Chemical Bonding**" incident in Chapter 1, where symbolic inclusion replaced mechanical redundancy.

- **The Texas Power Grid Collapse (2021):** A failure to winterize critical infrastructure during a push for "Transition" resulted in hundreds of deaths as the physics of the grid filed a verdict the state couldn't override.

II. The Institutional Failure: Competence vs. Compliance

- **The Medical Licensing Transition (2022):** The decision to move USMLE Step 1 to a Pass/Fail system removed the primary objective metric for physician competency. This mirrors the "**Tissue Aligners**" of Chapter 2 who prioritized "Auras" over anatomy.
- **The California Math Framework (2023):** The implementation of "Detracking" effectively removed advanced math for high-achievers under the guise of equity. This parallels the "**Banishing of the Riddle**" in Chapter 5.

III. The Economic Failure: The Joy Deficit

- **The Silicon Valley Bank Collapse (2023):** A management team focused heavily on ESG metrics and DEI initiatives while operating without a Chief Risk Officer during peak volatility. This is the real-world equivalent of the "**Vault of Silic**" investing gold in "Community Joy."

- **Retail Decollapse (Prop 47):** The effective decriminalization of theft in major urban centers led to the total withdrawal of commercial services. This mirrors the "**Unsanctioned Redistribution**" witnessed on the Bridge of Judges.

IV. The Social Failure: The Nursery of Spies

- **Washington Senate Bill 5599 (2023):** Legislation allowing the state to withhold children from parents who do not "affirm" specific ideological transitions. This creates a direct parallel to the "**Sept of Care**" taking Sia in Chapter 9.

Status of Case: TERMINAL. No further interventions recommended.

ABOUT THE AUTHOR

Operating under a pseudonym to speak freely, PRESTON GALT is a veteran financier with over three decades of experience at the highest levels of investment banking and global markets. Having witnessed the fragility of the financial system from the inside, he writes to expose the geometric truths that govern risk, ruin, and survival. He writes from the coast of Florida, watching the tide go out.

www.ingramcontent.com/pod-product-compliance
Lightning Source LLC
LaVergne TN
LVHW090535110826
845146LV00003B/1108

9798218929695